Anne of Green Gables

Stories for Young Readers

L. M. Montgomery
Adapted by Deirdre Kessler

∾ Illustrations by David Preston Smith ∾

NIMBUS
PUBLISHING

The girl was excited. She had come all the way to Prince Edward Island from Nova Scotia on the train to be adopted by Matthew and Marilla Cuthbert. Matthew and Marilla were brother and sister. Because they were getting old, they needed help with the work around their farm, Green Gables. Matthew's heart troubled him a good deal. They had decided to send to the orphanage for a boy.

When Matthew arrived at the station to pick up the boy they'd sent for, all he saw was a pale girl with red hair. The girl knew who he was, though, and went right up to him.

"I suppose you are Mr. Matthew Cuthbert of Green Gables?" she said in a clear, sweet voice. "Oh, it seems so wonderful that I'm going to live with you and belong to you. I've never belonged to anybody—not really."

Matthew was a very shy man. He was especially shy with girls and women. Except for his sister, Marilla, and his neighbour, Mrs. Rachel Lynde, he never spoke to women. But he liked this little girl already. He did not want to make her sad by telling her she could not stay with them at Green Gables.

"I'll let Marilla tell her there's been a mistake," he thought to himself as he shook the girl's scrawny little hand.

All the way home in the buggy the girl talked excitedly.

"People laugh at me because I use big words. But if you have big ideas you have to use big words to express them, haven't you?" she said.

"Well now, I dunno," said Matthew.

"I've always heard Prince Edward Island was the prettiest place in the world, and I used to imagine I was living here," she chattered to Matthew. "It's delightful when your imaginings come true, isn't it?"

"Well now, I dunno," said Matthew, who was enjoying himself very much.

"Mrs. Spencer said my tongue must be hung in the middle, I talk so much."

Matthew was beginning to dread the moment when the child would have to be told she could not stay at Green Gables. In the short time he had known her he had become quite fond of her. How disappointed she was going to be!

Chapter 2

"Where is the boy?"

Marilla looked at the odd little figure in the stiff, ugly dress, with the long braids of red hair, and the big glowing eyes.

"Matthew Cuthbert, who's that? Where is the boy?"

"There wasn't any boy," said Matthew. "There was only *her*."

"No boy! But there *must* have been a boy. We sent word to Mrs. Spencer to bring a boy!"

"You don't want me!" cried the child, dropping her worn-out suitcase. "You don't want me because I'm not a boy!

I might have expected it! Nobody ever did want me. Oh, what shall I do? This is the most *tragical* thing that ever happened to me! I'm going to burst into tears."

Burst into tears she did.

"Well, well, there's no need to cry so about it," said Marilla, who could see already that this was no ordinary child. "What's your name?"

"Anne Shirley. Anne spelled with an *e*."

Anne wanted to stay at Green Gables.

"If I was very beautiful would you keep me?" she asked Marilla.

"No. We want a boy to help Matthew on the farm. A girl would be of no use to us. We'll have to go see Mrs. Spencer tomorrow. You'll have to be sent back to the orphanage."

When Anne had gone upstairs to sleep, Matthew told Marilla how much he liked Anne. He wanted to keep her. She brought new life to Green Gables.

"I'm *not* going to keep her," were Marilla's final words that night.

Chapter 3

A Home of Her Own

The next morning Anne drove in the buggy with Marilla to White Sands to see Mrs. Spencer.

"Matthew and I clearly requested a boy," she told Mrs. Spencer. "There's been a mistake. This girl will have to be sent back to the orphanage."

"I don't think it will be necessary to send her back," replied Mrs. Spencer. "Mrs. Peter Blewett was up here yesterday. She was wishing she had a little girl to help her with all those quarrelsome children of hers. Anne could go live with her!"

Marilla had heard what a horrible temper Mrs. Blewett had. And how stingy she was. The idea of sending Anne to live with such an awful woman made Marilla's heart stir with pity. Poor Anne had been in so many dreadful homes in her short life.

Just then Mrs. Blewett appeared. She darted her eyes over Anne from head to foot. She pinched Anne's thin arm.

"How old are you and what's your name?" she demanded in a mean, horrible voice.

"I'd rather go back to the orphanage than go live with her," Anne whispered to Marilla. A lump came to her throat. Her eyes smarted from tears.

Marilla's heart softened. She decided to have Anne return with her to Green Gables temporarily to prevent Mrs. Blewett from taking her.

"I never in all my life saw or heard anything equal to this Anne-girl," Marilla muttered to herself. "She *is* kind of interesting, as Matthew says. I can feel already that I'm wondering what on earth she'll say next. She'll be casting a spell over me, too. She's cast it over Matthew. That look he gave me as we left for Mrs. Spencer's said everything. I wish he was more like other men and would talk things out. A body could answer back then and argue him into reason. But what's to be done with a man who just *looks*?"

Later, when Matthew and Marilla were out milking the cows, Marilla told her brother that Mrs. Blewett wanted to take Anne to live with her.

"I wouldn't give a dog I liked to that Blewett woman," said Matthew.

"I don't fancy her myself," Marilla said. "And there *is* something sweet about Anne. She's very smart. And I've got kind of used to the idea of keeping her. I've never brought up a child. I dare say I'll make a horrible mess of it. But I know you're dead set on keeping her. And she's a likable little thing, for all. So, as far as I'm concerned, she may stay."

"Well now, I reckoned you'd come to see it in that light, Marilla," said Matthew. His shy face glowed with delight.

Later, when Matthew and Marilla had returned to the house after milking the cows, Marilla said to Anne, "Well, Matthew and I have decided to keep you."

Anne's eyes filled with tears of joy. A home of her own! Finally, she had a home of her own!

Chapter 4

Mrs. Lynde

Anne had been in her new home for two weeks before she met up with a neighbour, Mrs. Rachel Lynde. In those two weeks she had explored every tree and stream and nook and cranny around Green Gables.

Mrs. Lynde was a busybody. She prided herself on always speaking her mind. She thought Marilla had done a foolish and risky thing by getting a strange orphan girl. She took one look at Anne and said: "Well, they didn't pick you for your looks, that's certain. Lawful heart, did anyone ever

see such freckles? You're thin as a rail. And hair as red as carrots!"

With one bound Anne crossed the kitchen floor and stood before Mrs. Lynde.

"I hate you! I hate you — I hate you! How *dare* you call me skinny and ugly? How would *you* like to be told that you are FAT and CLUMSY? I don't care if I hurt your feelings. You have hurt mine worse than they were ever hurt before. And I'll *never* forgive you for it, never, never!"

Mrs. Lynde was shocked. Marilla sent Anne upstairs to her room. Secretly Matthew was happy that someone had finally told off the old lady. Marilla was sorry that Anne had acted so badly, but she said, "You were too hard on her, Rachel."

This was too much for Mrs. Lynde. She swept out of the house and away.

Marilla went upstairs to speak with Anne.

"You were rude and saucy. You must go to Mrs. Lynde and tell her you are very sorry for your bad temper. You must ask her to forgive you."

Anne stayed in her room all that night. And she stayed there all the next day. She was determined *never* to apologize to Mrs. Lynde. But the next evening Matthew tiptoed to Anne's room and got her to agree to apologize, even if she didn't really mean it.

Anne set to work on making up a long apology. Then she marched downstairs, told Marilla she was ready, and the two of them set off to Mrs. Lynde's house.

"Oh, Mrs. Lynde," Anne said with a quiver in her voice.

"It was very wicked of me to fly into a temper because you told me the truth. My hair *is* red and I *am* freckled and skinny and ugly. What I said about *you* is true, too, but I shouldn't have said it. Please, please forgive me, Mrs. Lynde."

"There, there, child," said the old gossip. "Of course I forgive you." There were tears in Mrs. Lynde's eyes.

Anne did not let on that she was enjoying very much making such a long and good apology. Marilla hid a smile.

Chapter 5

Kindred Spirits

"Anne," said Marilla. "I'm going to see Mrs. Barry to borrow a skirt pattern. If you like you can come along with me and meet her little girl Diana. Diana is just your age. You must be polite and well-behaved."

"But—oh, Marilla—I'm so frightened! What if she shouldn't like me? It would be the most *tragical disappointment* in my life!"

"I do wish you wouldn't use such long words. It sounds so funny in a little girl. Now, come along, Anne."

They went over to Orchard Slope by the shortcut. Mrs. Barry met them at her kitchen door. Mrs. Barry was a rather stern woman.

"How do you do?" she said. "Come in. This is my little girl, Diana. Why don't you two go out into the garden?"

Outside Anne and Diana stood looking shyly at each other. Diana was very pretty. She had black eyes and black hair, rosy cheeks, and a merry expression on her face.

"Oh, Diana!" said Anne at last. "Will you be my friend for ever and ever?"

"You're an odd girl, Anne. I heard before that you were odd. But I believe I'm going to like you real well."

"We're *kindred spirits*," Anne told Marilla on the way home. "And — oh, Marilla — Diana said there's going to be a Sunday school picnic next week. They're going to make ice cream! I have never tasted ice cream. Diana tried to explain what it was like, but I guess ice cream is one of those things that is beyond my imagination. Please can I go? Marilla, can I go to it? I've dreamed of picnics, but I've never…"

"Yes, child, you can go."

Anne threw her arms around Marilla's neck and kissed her.

"There, there, never mind your kissing nonsense. Now, get out your patchwork and have your square done before tea time."

Chapter 6

~: ✳ :~

Avonlea School

"I think I'm going to like school here," Anne announced to Matthew and Marilla after her first day at Avonlea School. "I don't think that much of the teacher, though."

"Anne Shirley, don't let me hear you talking about your teacher in that way again," Marilla said sharply.

Three weeks went by smoothly. Anne made friends with all the little girls at Avonlea School.

"Gilbert Blythe will be in school today, Anne. He's good-looking *and* smart. Oh — there he is!" Diana pointed to a tall, curly-haired boy, who nodded hello and winked at Anne.

"I think your Gilbert Blythe is handsome," whispered Anne. "But he's very bold. It isn't good manners to wink at a strange girl."

That morning in school Anne sat with her chin propped in her hand and daydreamed. She did not notice Gilbert trying to get her attention. He was not used to being ignored by girls. All the Avonlea girls liked him. Finally, Gilbert reached across the aisle, picked up the end of Anne's long red braid, and said in a piercing whisper:

"CARROTS! CARROTS!"

Anne sprang to her feet.

"You mean, hateful boy!" she exclaimed angrily. "How dare you!"

THWACK! She brought her slate down on Gilbert's head.

Everyone stared with open mouths at Anne. Tommy Sloan let his team of crickets escape—they hopped away down the aisle dragging their harness of horsehair.

"Anne Shirley, what have you done?" Mr. Phillips said in a stern, angry voice.

Gilbert spoke up. "It was my fault, Mr. Phillips. I teased her."

Mr. Phillips paid no attention to Gilbert. He made Anne stand in front of the class for the rest of the afternoon. On the chalkboard he wrote: *Ann Shirley has a very bad temper.* To make matters worse, he spelled Anne without an *e*.

When school was dismissed, Gilbert Blythe tried to stop Anne as she was leaving.

"I'm awfully sorry I made fun of your hair, Anne," he said. "Honest I am. Don't be angry with me, please."

Anne walked right by him and found Diana in the schoolyard.

"Diana, I shall never forgive Gilbert Blythe."

Anne made up her mind to hate Gilbert Blythe to the end of her life.

Chapter 7

Trouble at an Afternoon Tea

"I'll be driving over to Carmody to a meeting this afternoon and I won't likely be home before dark. Anne, you'll have to make supper for Matthew, and—well, it may be spoiling you, but—you can ask Diana to come over to spend the afternoon with you and have tea here. There's fruitcake and a bottle of raspberry cordial you can have. The cordial's on the second shelf in the cupboard."

That afternoon Diana knocked on the door at Green Gables. Prim and proper, the two girls shook hands and

Chapter 8

Anne Saves Minnie May

One night when Marilla and Mrs. Lynde had gone to Charlottetown, Matthew and Anne sat in the cozy kitchen at Green Gables. Anne was studying geometry so that she could beat Gilbert at it the next day in school. Matthew dozed in the rocking chair. All of a sudden the door was flung open and in rushed Diana Barry, white-faced and breathless.

"Oh, Anne, do come quick," said Diana nervously. "My little sister Minnie May is awful sick. She's got croup. My

Just then, Gilbert Blythe came rowing toward her.

"Anne Shirley! How on earth did you get there?" He pulled close to the post and reached out his hand. Anne, clinging to Gilbert, scrambled down into his boat. "What happened, Anne?"

"We were playing Elaine. Will you be kind enough to row me to the landing?"

Gilbert rowed her to shore.

"I'm very much obliged to you," Anne said coldly.

"Anne, look here. Can't we be good friends? I'm awfully sorry I made fun of your hair that time. I only meant it for a joke. Besides, it's so long ago. I think your hair is awfully pretty now—honest I do. Let's be friends."

For a second Anne hesitated. Then her old hate welled up inside her.

"No. I shall never be friends with you, Gilbert Blythe."

"All right! I'll *never* ask you to be friends again, Anne Shirley." Gilbert turned angrily and rowed away.

Anne watched him go. She almost wished she had answered him differently. She sat down and had a good cry.

Chapter 10

Anne Wins a Prize

"Anne," said Marilla, "Miss Stacy was here this afternoon. She came to ask Matthew and me if we would like you to join a special class of her good students. You would be studying for an examination to get you into Queen's College to study for being a teacher."

"Oh, Marilla! It's my life's dream come true. But won't it be dreadfully expensive? Mr. Andrews says it cost him one hundred and fifty dollars to put Prissy through Queen's."

"Matthew and I decided long ago we would do the best

we could for you. So if you want to join the Queen's class, you may."

"Oh, Marilla, thank you." Anne flung her arms around Marilla's waist. "I'm grateful to you and Matthew. I'll study hard as I can and do my best to make you proud of me."

The winter came and went. For Anne the days slipped by like golden beads on the necklace of the year. She was happy. Anne and Diana grew. They were no longer little girls.

The summer passed and a new year at school began. Matthew had a bad spell with his heart, but Marilla decided not to tell Anne about it. She did not want to worry Anne, who was studying very hard to pass the Queen's examination.

Marilla felt a queer regret over Anne's growing up. When Matthew came in from the barn one night he heard Marilla sobbing.

"I was thinking about Anne," she explained. "She's got to be such a big girl—and she'll probably be away from us next winter. I'll miss her terribly."

"Well now, she'll be able to come home often," comforted Matthew.

"It won't be the same thing as having her here all the time," sighed Marilla gloomily.

At the end of June, Anne and Gilbert and students from all over the Island gathered in Charlottetown to take the difficult Queen's entrance exams. Then for three dreadful weeks they waited for the pass list to be printed in the newspaper.

One evening, Diana came running.

"Anne, you've passed—passed the *very first*—you and Gilbert both—you've tied—but your name is first. Oh, I'm so proud!"

They hurried to the hayfield where Matthew was working. Mrs. Lynde was talking to Marilla at the fence.

"Oh, Matthew! I've passed and I'm first!"

Something warm and pleasant welled up in the hearts of the old brother and sister.

"Well now, I always said it. I knew you could beat them all easy." Matthew's heart was glad.

"You've done pretty well, I must say, Anne," said Marilla, trying to hide her extreme pride from Mrs. Lynde.

"I just guess she has done well," said Mrs. Lynde. "You're a credit to your friends, Anne, and we're all proud of you."

Chapter 11

Matthew's Girl

The next weeks were busy ones at Green Gables. Anne was getting ready to go to Queen's College in Charlottetown. Neither Matthew nor Marilla could imagine life at Green Gables without Anne. One night, Matthew got up and went out-of-doors. His eyes were moist. Alone under the stars of the blue summer night he said, "Well now, I guess there never was a luckier mistake than when Mrs. Spencer sent us a girl rather than a boy. I mean when she sent Anne."

Anne left to begin her year's study to become a teacher. Gilbert Blythe would be the only one in her class she knew. Not that she ever so much as spoke to him.

In the spring, Matthew and Marilla drove all the way to Charlottetown to see Anne graduate. She had won a four-year scholarship to college. The three returned to Avonlea. Anne looked forward to seeing Diana and to spending a whole wonderful summer at Green Gables.

The next morning at breakfast it suddenly struck Anne that Matthew was not looking well. Surely he was much greyer than he had been a year before.

"No, he isn't well," said Marilla. "He's had some real bad spells with his heart this spring. I've been real worried about him. I'm hoping he'll be better now we've got a good hired man. And, Anne, you always cheer him up."

"You've been working too hard today, Matthew," Anne told him when they went for the cows that evening. "Why won't you take things easier?"

"Well now, I can't seem to. It's only that I'm getting old, Anne, and keep forgetting to take things easier."

"If I had been the boy you sent for," said Anne, "I'd be able to help you so much now and spare you in a hundred ways."

"I guess it wasn't a *boy* that took the scholarship, was it? It was a girl—*my girl*. And I'd rather have you than a dozen boys," said Matthew, patting her hand. He smiled his shy smile at her as he went into the yard.

Anne took the memory of that smile with her when she went to her room that night. It was the last night before sorrow touched Anne's life.

Chapter 12

Marilla and Anne Alone

"MATTHEW—MATTHEW—what is the matter? Matthew, are you sick?"

It was Marilla who spoke. Anne came through the hall in time to see Matthew standing in the porch doorway. His face was strange and grey. Anne and Marilla leapt across the kitchen to him at the same moment. Before they could reach him Matthew had fallen to the floor.

"He's fainted," gasped Marilla. "Anne—run for Martin. Quick, quick!"

Martin, the hired man, started at once for the doctor, stopping at the Barrys' house on his way. Mrs. Lynde was there on an errand. Mrs. Lynde and the Barrys rushed to Green Gables.

Mrs. Lynde pushed Anne and Marilla gently aside, tried Matthew's pulse, and then lay her ear over his heart. She looked at their faces sorrowfully and tears came into her eyes.

"Oh, Marilla," she said gravely, "I don't think…we can do anything for him."

"Mrs. Lynde, you don't think—you can't think Matthew is…is…." Anne could not say the dreadful word. She turned sick and pale.

"Child, yes, I'm afraid of it. Look at his face. When you've seen that look as often as I have you'll know what it means."

The news spread quickly through Avonlea. All day friends and neighbours gathered at Green Gables.

When night came softly over Green Gables, the old house was hushed. In the parlour lay Matthew Cuthbert in his coffin. There was a kindly smile on his calm face, as if he slept, dreaming pleasant dreams. Anne wept her heart out.

"There, there, don't cry so, dearie," said Marilla. "It can't bring him back. We've got each other. Oh, Anne, I love you as if you were my own flesh and blood and you've been my joy ever since you came to Green Gables."

Two days afterwards they carried Matthew Cuthbert over his homestead threshold and away from the fields he had plowed and the orchards he had loved.

Chapter 13

Good Enemies Become Good Friends

Life at Green Gables slipped back into its old groove, until one day when Marilla returned from town and sat sadly at the kitchen table.

"Anne, I'll have to sell Green Gables. I've been to the bank. I've thought it all over. The buildings are old and need repair and the land needs farming. I can't do it alone. With you gone to college, I'd go crazy with trouble and loneliness."

"You *mustn't* sell Green Gables!" cried Anne. "You surely don't think I could leave you alone in your trouble after all you've done for me. I'm not going to college. I have decided to stay at home. My mind is quite made up, so don't argue with me. I'll teach school in Carmody because Gil—I mean, someone else is teaching at the Avonlea School. And I'll study on my own. Oh—I have it all planned out, Marilla. I'll read to you and keep you cheered up. And we'll be real cozy and happy here together, you and I."

"You're a dear and thoughtful young lady," said Marilla, relieved to know she would not have to leave her beloved Green Gables after all. Marilla and Anne sat in companionable silence for a while, then Marilla spoke again.

"What a nice-looking fellow Gilbert Blythe is. So tall and manly. He looks a lot like his father did at the same age. You know, John Blythe and I used to be real good friends. People called him my beau."

Anne was very surprised. She could not imagine Marilla having a boyfriend.

"Oh, Marilla—what happened? Why didn't you…?"

"We had a quarrel. I wouldn't forgive him when he asked me to. I meant to, after a while—but I was sulky and angry and I wanted to punish him first. He never came back. But I always felt sorry. I've always kind of wished I'd forgiven him when I had the chance."

It was a warm evening. Anne and Marilla sat on a stone bench by the front door. They saw Mrs. Lynde hurrying up the lane. She had some gossip to share with them.

"I just guess you're going to teach school right here in Avonlea," she said. "As soon as Gilbert Blythe heard that you were staying at Green Gables he went right to the trustees. He gave up the school just for you. I must say it was real kind and thoughtful of him."

The next evening Anne saw a tall lad come whistling along the lane. It was Gilbert. The whistle died on his lips when he saw Anne. He lifted his cap politely, but would have passed on in silence if Anne had not stopped him and held out her hand.

"Gilbert," she said, her cheeks growing red, "I want to thank you for giving up the school for me. It was very good of you and I want you to know I appreciate it."

Gilbert took her hand.

"It wasn't particularly good of me at all, Anne. Are we going to be friends after this? Have you really forgiven me my old faults?"

Anne laughed. "I forgave you that day at the pond, although I didn't know it. What a stubborn little goose I was. I've been sorry ever since."

"We *are* going to be the best of friends," said Gilbert happily. "We were born to be good friends, Anne. I know we can help each other in many ways. You are going to keep up your studies, aren't you? So am I. Come, I'm going to walk home with you."

Marilla looked curiously at Anne when she walked into the kitchen.

"Was that Gilbert Blythe who came up the lane with you, Anne?"

"Yes, it was Gilbert," answered Anne, vexed to find herself blushing.

"I didn't think you and Gilbert Blythe were such good

friends that you'd stand for half an hour at the gate talking to him," said Marilla, with a dry smile.

"We haven't been—we've been good enemies. But we have decided that it will be much more sensible to be good friends in future."

Anne sat long at her window that night. The wind purred softly in the cherry trees. Stars twinkled over the pointed firs in the hollow. Diana's light gleamed through the woods.

"God's in his heaven, all's right with the world," whispered Anne softly.